at The Crossing With Denis McShane

William Allen Knight

BIBLIOLIFE

AT THE CROSSING
WITH DENIS McSHANE

BY

WILLIAM ALLEN KNIGHT

AUTHOR OF

"THE SONG OF OUR SYRIAN GUEST"
ETC.

DRAWINGS BY
FLORENCE SCOVEL SHINN

THE PILGRIM PRESS

BOSTON   NEW YORK   CHICAGO
MCMXII

CONTENTS

AT THE CROSSING
WITH DENIS McSHANE

BEFORE A CERTAIN JUNE DAY

"MORNIN', your Riv'rence."

My first impression was that the old street sweeper had somehow mistaken the Domine for Father O'Leary. He had always seemed a dull enough figure to do the like; besides, I noticed that he squinted hard when he shuffled aside for a passing team. But my companion on the sidewalk shut off that exit from my amused surprise.

"Good morning, good morning, Mr. McShane. A fine morning, too, isn't it?"

"Indade it is, sir, thank God."

"The shower last night helped

you a bit, Denis, for a clean street today, I hope."

"Sure, sure, Father — ur-r-r, your Riv'rence — God be praised."

Clearly Denis McShane knew well enough that he was not talking with Father O'Leary. Yet his greeting had been marked by as pretty an exhibition of heartsome deportment, I fancy, as the human drama anywhere exhibited at that moment under the sky. Stopping the swing of his long switch broom, he straightened his body to its limit of uprightness, slowly faced about, and touched his weathered hat, smiling and blinking in the June sunshine. And while he stood leaning on his broom handle the little colloquy already reported gave proof of habitual amenities between Denis and the Domine, demonstrating their friendship in much the same fashion as the roses in dooryards round about testified that it was Junetime.

The old Irishman, though long a

familiar figure in our street, had
seemed to my eyes so impersonal or
at least of another order of being
that I was almost as much surprised
as if the milkman's drowsing gray
mare had upraised her head and
whinnied to the Domine. For you
must know that this title, in the
speech of Morningdale, was the des-
ignation for the man who had grown
gray in the pastorate of First Church,
and Denis was — it sounds strange
now to repeat the oldtime epithet!
— a papist.

To be sure, everybody in Morningdale respected the Domine; indeed, nearly everybody loved him
—that is, speaking after our wont,
everybody of our kind, by which
we meant of our Protestant stock.
He had fondly married most of us
who were in mid-life or younger,
baptized our little ones on pleasant
Sundays, buried our dead in all
weathers; and withal we had never
seen his like for being a friend to

the whole village in times of need. But we had yet to learn the scope of his capacity for friendliness.

In truth, he had been something of a puzzle to us from the first, he was so given to serene unexpectedness. Not least among his queer propensities in our eyes as the years went on was an apparent fondness for the Irish. There had been ample occasion for perplexity over that matter. For the sons and daughters of Erin seemed somehow to have found their Paradise in our town.

"Why, they are humans," the Domine would say when we voiced our dismay, "exceedingly interesting specimens of the *genus homo*, in fact. Let me see — who was it that made of one blood all nations of men for to dwell on all the face of the earth?"

"It beats a', that!" said Duncan McGregor, our Bible class leader, whose Scotch head was making the best of our un-Presbyterian church.

Once in a class discussion he solemnly added: "But what saith the Boohk — what saith it further? Finish the passage." Then he did it himself with impressive precision — "'and hath determined the times before appointed, and the bounds of their habitation,' aye, 'the bounds of their habitation.'" This seemed a master-stroke, indeed.

When some one told the Domine thereof, a twinkling in his eyes heralded a rejoinder which became famous in Morningdale. "Anyway," said he, "I am glad that Duncan did not see fit to apply this clause to his side of the Irish Sea." The dear fellow was invulnerably friendly to all.

At length the neighboring city reached out a long arm and took us into its bounds. Then the appropriation of Morningdale proceeded apace. Irish bluecoats sauntered through our streets, pausing jauntily to chat at our back doors with

Irish maids. Irish postmen took
charge of our letters with good-
natured quickness of understanding
as to the significance of postmarks
or the handwriting of addresses
thereon. One by one village stores
blossomed out with comely colleens
behind the counters. Of a Sunday
morning we Puritan folk heard the
patter of brisk feet on the sidewalk
while yet we were indulging in the
extra Sabbath nap; and when we
were on the way to First Church
with the ancient bell ding-donging
the last strokes, the streets of Morningdale were black — the men being many — with home-going Irish
humanity, or gay as a garden with
white garments and bright colors
by reason of the abounding maiden-
hood, all pouring out at the doors of
St. Anne's.

We shook our heads, thinking
much but saying little. What could
we say? But our hearts were
murky.

With Denis McShane

In such a plight, judge how it tested our confidence to hear reports at length that the Domine was a favorite with these swarming aliens. We knew that they were wrong who declared that he was "a Jesuit in disguise." That charge had a fickle vogue in the days of an agitation designated by certain letters, three in number and usually spoken with grave eyes. But a Jesuit would hardly include a bride in his disguise outfit, we reasoned; and the Domine's wife, by grace of the passing years, had proved an altogether substantial reality, being obviously dearer to him even than she was to us. This little lady quite effectually checked the spread of that mental pestilence, and at last by her serene wifeliness exorcised all terrors raised by such a delirium of fevered minds.

Besides that, we could not forget what the Domine did once when our choir, by some inadvertence as to the words accompanying music that

pleased them, sang an *Ave Maria*
in plain English. After they had
sounded forth for the second time
some such refrain as

"Thou who openest for us salvation,
Holy Mother, pray for us!"

he leaned over the choir rail back
of the pulpit and whispered something that made them — well, we
were never able to settle the question as to what did happen precisely, and I must not take the risk
of reopening that memorable discussion in First Church Parish. It
is enough to say that they stopped
singing, and the Domine rather suddenly and resonantly gave out the
hymn,

"All hail the power of Jesus' name,"

adding the somewhat superfluous
injunction, "To the tune *Corona-
tion*, brethren." At this distance
perhaps it may be safely stated further that the choir's friendship for

the Domine proved strong enough
to outride and at length allay the
tempest of rather inconsistent crit-
icism which might — who knows the
ways of the winds? — even have set
the good man adrift from his anchor-
age in Morningdale.

No, he was not in any wise weak
in his Protestant proclivities. And
yet there was no denying that there
was some warrant for the reports
that our Irish neighbors were actually friends of the Domine. What
could it mean? Everybody knew
that he and Father O'Leary were
so joined together in fighting the
devil and all his works, particularly
the barrooms, that they seemed to
have forgot all about fighting one
another. For my part 1 suspected
that this had not a little to do with
the way the people of St. Anne's
bore themselves toward our Domine; for Father O'Leary was a ma-
jor among his parishioners, small of
stature though he was, and they

obeyed as well as loved him. But be that as it may, the reports continued.

Somehow I had failed to see these Morningdale small matters other than as the ways of a man ever doing the unexpected out of sheer good nature and human fulness. That our Domine's relations with the Irish had to do in any manner with the cause of the Most High in the earth, that he was bridging a chasm in the King's name, yes, for the feet of the King's men, never occurred to me until that morning when Denis McShane stood at the crossing, transfigured before my eyes by the June glory and the bright light of human kindness.

I can see the stocky old figure now, his face beaming, his horny hand upraised to his hat, his switch broom bent as it bore his leaning weight, and the shimmer of fragrant sunshine round him. His quiet brogue is in my ear still. Many a

time since then, for the sole purpose
of hearing the same, have I passed
where I saw him swinging his broom.
So it was that Denis and I became
friends at length.

He is gone now; no more is he
seen swaying slowly adown the
street. And the Domine is gone,
too. I may tell what I will. Father
O'Leary will not chide me, I know,
if the things I write should ever
reach the rectory of St. Anne's.

II

SOME MORNINGDALE MAT-
TERS AFTERWARD

AFTER that memorable June day
when I saw at the street crossing the
glorification of Denis McShane —
that is the right word, the scene
shines so bright through the haze
of the years — I found myself taking strange interest, akin to delight,
in observing the Domine's ways with
our Irish neighbors. Or perhaps it
would be more exact to say their
ways with him; for he never seemed
to do more than be responsive to
some instinctive, human understanding on their part.

It was fine to walk the street at
his side and watch Irish little fel-
lows jerk their caps to him with
respectful glances. Many a time I
heard a bunch of lads from the paro-

LITTLE MAIDENS ON CONFIRMATION
SUNDAY

chial school call out, "Good mornin',
Minister!" That was the Catholic
title for him — minister. I won-
dered at it; for we seldom used it
ourselves in daily speech, and yet
it was the most fitting term in the
language for him, this man who
ministered to all Morningdale.

And the faces of Irish girls —
from the little maidens, on Confirmation Sunday pretty as apple blos-
soms with their white veils, white
garments even to their stockings,
and their red cheeks, to Miss
Maloney who was "head sales-
lady" at the dry goods store —all
lighted with the gleam of Erin's
smiles as they saw him approaching
and watched for his recognition. I
came to feel that I would give half
the village lots left me by the hon-
ored pillar of First Church who was
my father, if thereby I might have
the music of such simple gladness
sounding for me as their voices in
greeting made for the Domine!

At the Crossing

No matter how the water-wagon driver might skimp the dusty highway elsewhere, it was always abundantly sprinkled before the parsonage on a summer's day; and if the snow-plow chanced to shunt so as to leave a bank on the Domine's walk, it was actually turned back to clear a path, even as it was before the rectory of St. Anne's. Day laborers lounging at nightfall in a corner group would still their ebullient chatting to say "Good evenin', Docthor," or some such sudden shift to the language of respect, touching their headpieces as he passed with a pleasant response. I used to see Irish policemen salute him — a lone stroller on his uneventful beat, a whole squad tramping heavily from headquarters to their night-watch — and it was as when soldiers happen to pass a general on the field.

Even Mike Finnigan, no matter how busy he might be, would promptly come outside any time if he saw the Domine standing before his saloon door; and Mike would give his word and keep it, too, when the Domine named some man who was making a beast of himself and said, "I have sent him to Father O'Leary to sign the pledge; now, not another drink to him, Mr. Finnigan — give me your hand on that." There was a growing list of sober workmen in Morningdale because of those pacts.

"He's white," was Mike's comment when he reappeared behind the bar.

"He'd shut you up tomorrow, though, if he could, Finnigan," some toper would vouchsafe, grinning over his glass.

"Sure — an' what's more, him an' Father O'Leary'll do it some day, an' put that in your pipe fur a cool smoke! What wuz it you'll have, Tim Shaughnessey?"

But what pleased me most of

all, though it touched that source of
waters a man would fain keep un-
reached, occurred at Grandma Goodman's funeral — she who was the
oldest member of First Church and
had a head of her own to the last.

The Domine had said his last
word. The throng of First Church
folk had passed out to the dooryard
and autumn's russet mellowness.
The large circle of family kin had
taken their leave of the saintly form
to the third generation of them it
had lapped. The Domine stood
alone beside the bier banked in
flowers, we pall-bearers awaiting his
nod. He was in no hurry about
bearing *her* out from that home —
forever!

I saw him glance toward the open
door as in reverie. Suddenly his
attention was drawn. He beckoned.
Then he stepped to the waiting
threshold and spoke to an old Irish
woman who was standing apart
outside — in the shelter of a trumpet

honeysuckle vine, the trumpets deep scarlet. Soon she came tiptoeing beside him to where the body of Grandma Goodman lay. The Domine turned and whispered to the waiting undertaker while she bent reverently over the opening in the coffin.

I saw her lay a soft touch on the folded white hands, smoothing the ruches also; then — none being near, none seeing, as she supposed — I saw her reach forth two old fingers, saw her swiftly, secretly make the sign of the Cross on the white-haired, cold brow, saw her lips move with still breathings as of words. Then she turned and with body bent tiptoed away.

Tears came nearer brimming my eyes at that sight than I like to have them. Alone, standing where her priest might not come, for love's sake she had outstretched as he did two fingers, two toil-worn fingers of her own, with a whispered something surely prayer-laden! Doing

the little she could that she might
somehow impart the saving help of
her Church to Grandma — she who
had washed the family clothes and
made them white in her suds for a
generation!

It was Mrs. McShane.

Let none who may chance to scan
this breast-bare narrative of Morningdale matters as seen by one who
was a part of all he saw, suspect me
of blurring the differences between
our Catholic neighbors and ourselves
because of the glamour thrown over
all by the Domine's ways. I am
the son of my father, as all who
know me seem to find reason for
saying evermore — whether it be
in the uplift of my hand as I talk,
or the bald spot starting seasonably
on the crown of my head amidst
abundant hair elsewhere, or the way
I have of smiling and yet holding
fast to my own notion against all
comers. And my father, mark you,

besides having a keen relish for the
difference between the forms of god-
liness and the power thereof, was
exceedingly fond of the idea that we
are all kings and priests unto God.

Yet it was quite the way of my
father to detect essentials persist-
ing under differences whether due
to temperament, race qualities, life
conditions present or past, or any
other such cause of the ripples, still
pools, shallows, cascades, or deeps
found in the sea-going streams of
mankind's life. Moreover, it was
precisely like him to feel the charm
of all human graces regardless of
station or lot. He reveled in dis-
coveries of likenesses that divulge
kinships between every people and
tongue. I even remember the hush
in his voice and the glisten in his
eyes when he watched the parental
doings of some woodland creature or
harked to the variant-keyed song of
the hermit thrush as it sought to
sound somehow its instinctive feel-

ings amidst the sanctities of evening time. "How like us men, after
all!" he would whisper.

That thrush song, now sung in
one key, then in another and still
another, but much the same in all,
was his favorite likeness, I think,
in the whole of nature to man's ways
in love and worship.

All these things, be it known,
were true of his son.

In the sunshine of the Domine's in-
fluence, therefore, the years brought
forth and matured a friendship
with Denis McShane in my own
right, ripening the fruit thereof at
last. No tree in the orchard flank-
ing our house-garden — many of
them planted in my father's early
prime, and grafted afresh as his
years mounted that they might
match his unspent and richening
manhood, some of them more beautiful to me now than the color or fra-
grance of blossom and fruit ever
made them, because I remembered

summer or autumn days when my
mother's face looked up through
their leaves while her agile boy
dropped a choice Harvest Sweet
or Baldwin into her dear apron —
no tree in my orchard yielded me
pleasanter returns than my friendship with the old street sweeper.
For there is no pleasure in life
as a man nears the September of
his days more—shall I say tooth-
some?—more like ripe apples when
autumn comes, than the mellow at-
tachments of the lowly whom one
has befriended.

I daily received his greeting from
the street, though he seemed un-
aware of most passers-by; flavorous
and racy were the chats we had when
I paused on the curb now and then.
By and by my delight in rehearsing
these things brought it to pass that
when my daughters were making
ready their Christmas gifts, Denis
— he had no children of his own,
by some unwonted quirk of Nature

in her ways with the Irish — Denis
and his wife were always remembered by the girls, their mother
aiding and abetting. They would
send a mother-of-pearl cross I had
brought from Bethlehem, or a string
of beads which their own timid
hands had thrust into that cavity
in Ste. Genevieve's tomb where
souvenirs are blest by the ashes of
the patron saint of Paris. "From
the Church of St. Mary the Virgin"
or "From the Church of St. Etienne,"
they would inscribe the gift, trusting
Mr. and Mrs. McShane to see some
delicate compliment to their own St.
Anne's. And Denis would be sure
to appear at our back door bearing
a bit of Irish lace, say, with Mrs.
McShane's "Merry Christmas," quite
matching my daughters, I thought,
in suiting the gift to the hearts of
the receivers.

When Mrs. McShane died we
sent flowers; and if Denis was looking out from behind the drawn

curtains of the livery carriage as
the morning procession took its
way from St. Anne's, he might have
seen me standing among the folk
that lined the sidewalk. My hat
was removed, my head bowed, as
every man's was in the throng of
Denis McShane's friends.

While the evening of that day
darkened on Morningdale I could
not do other than make my way
to his small dwelling. We sat together awhile — out on the bench
among geraniums that Mrs. Mc-
Shane had planted, under sun-
flowers that bent their heavy heads
down as if mournful and dumb with
Denis. I will not try to record
what I said. It was halting enough
to be left behind, though I did the
best I could. This only need be
told, that not once did I see the glow
of the old man's pipe in the gloam-
ing. This solace of his day's end
for a lifetime was in his hand; but
it was stone-cold all evening.

III

DENIS AND THE GIPSY

THE best of friends must be pre-
pared to discover at times that one
or the other has a secret — nothing
of consequence, perhaps, but something he wishes to keep to himself.
Friendship has few finer tokens than
to honor that wish outright. I had
occasion to remember this more
than once in my long relations with
the old street sweeper; and this I
did on that summer night when he
was first alone; for I noticed that
he kept looking momentarily at a
brass ring he always wore. But I
asked no questions.

There was one small matter, however, often the subject of my curiosity through the years, which I
became eager to learn about. Indeed, when I observed it still after

With Denis McShane

Mrs. McShane was gone, my curiosity deepened to tender longing. Was Denis really singing as he swung his broom through the street? Many a time I had thought that I caught the sound of song; and, believe me, I seemed to hear the same in the long autumnal days whose shining covered Denis McShane in the street — and his old wife's grave among the hillside crosses.

But though he seemed quite heedless of pedestrians in general, and usually stepped aside at the sound of a vehicle in good season without so much as glancing toward it, yet the monotone as of song was always hushed before I was near enough to listen. When I called my good morning or stopped on the curb, the old man would turn slowly and give me greeting as out of perfect silence — God bless him for the gleam and twinkle in his stolid face!

But there came a day when I

could not refrain in this alluring
matter. There was a light snowfall
that morning and perhaps for this
reason he did not hear my tread.
If the whole truth must be told, I
had stepped a bit softly to help the
snow's silencing. Besides, the early
December street was slushy and
rather heavy for his broom, which
doubtless gave Denis cause for being
more engaged than common, even
requiring the use of the noisier hoe.
And withal, Denis McShane was
age-bound indeed in those wifeless
days.

In any case, I stood listening —
stood so near that I heard his voice
distinctly — heard a rhythmic monotone, an old man's humdrum way
of singing, as he swayed and swayed
swinging his broom or dragging the
hoe over the stones.

It was so fine a thing — this
charming an unsavory and dreary
task by tuneful musings which no
doubt brought memory's sweet

silences round his bent head — that I came near leaving the veteran soul undisturbed, as one might a kneeling figure fingering magic beads before a wayside shrine.

But just as I was starting to pass on, he chanced to pause and stood half erect, one hand on his broom handle, the other on the hoe, while he scanned the street in leisurely obliviousness. Thus it was that he spied me at the curb. His face broke into quizzical beaming.

"Be all the saints!" He slowly swung the switch broom over his shoulder.

Sunlight on the fresh snow threw a sheen over all December's pallid beauty round about us. I remember how that setting seemed to befit the aged figure with the shining, quiet face.

"You and the sun will soon clear away the snow, Mr. McShane — I was watching you work together."

"Ach! Bedad, that's sure —

this wone, sir, please God. But the next — and the next! — But Christmas comes in snowtime, sir."

"That's a fact. And are you, too, thinking of Christmas so soon? Some girls I know were speaking of it only last night — and of you, Mr. McShane." I thought to buttress his loneliness by this slight treachery as to my daughters.

He caught the sound of a wagon yet a block away and slowly trudged to the curbing dragging the hoe. He eyed the rattling wheels as they came and passed.

"Thim gives me time," he mused beside me; "but these oty-mow-bills — faith! the things comes on a man shtill an' quick as the divil himself!"

One of these yet disquieting innovators in Morningdale at the time of which I am writing, sped by on muffled wheels before his words were followed by further speech. It was my opportunity.

"Would you mind my asking, Mr. McShane, if you were thinking of Christmas while you were singing?"

"Singin'?" He peered into my eyes gravely.

"I thought I heard you singing to yourself while you worked."

"Ach! 'Twas niver a bit of a tyune, sir, sure now. The likes o' me! — Sure, the song in me vaice left me this twinty year gone like the robins when the leaves is turnin' an' the nests is empty — they only chirps then, sir."

I marked a flicker of Irish humor in his steadfast gaze.

"I wouldn't say, though, that the old birds might not *feel* like singin', even when they only chirps a bit to thimselves."

Before long my eagerness prevailed, and the old man was repeating for me the words he was sounding while he worked. The lilt in his voice and the music of the words

were so like song in all save the
wing-way of melody that I readily
believed he spoke truly in declaring
that there was no "tyune" lifting
his utterance when I overheard him.
It was, however, like the singing of
primitive man, after all.

The only lines I can recall now
ran somewhat as follows:

"And brighter than the berries are the
    kindly Irish eyes,
  And cheery are the greetings of the
    day —
 The greetings and the blessings from the
    Irish hearts that rise
  At Christmas-time in Ireland far away."

"But what set you thinking of
Christmas now?" I asked with delight, when the slight teeter of his
whole frame with the pulsing words
had ceased.

"Why, 'tis Advent, sir, an' the
collect last Sunday wuz, 'Stir up
our hearts, O Lord, to make ready
the ways of thine only-begotten

Son!' An' Father O'Leary he says
to us, says he, 'A man should tyune
up his mind like a instrument o'
music.' We gets unstrung like a
fiddle in wet weather, he told us;
young wones is like new an' needs
tyunin' awful bad, bein' full o' sap
or sich like, an' old wones mustn't
git the notion they niver can do it
agin — ''old fiddles well tyuned
makes the best music of all,' he says.
So I wuz sayin' over thim words,
sir, to quit feelin' too old fur Christmas. An' you thought I wuz
singin'? Well, well, now!''

I knew enough to follow the vein
that had yielded such a nugget. We
talked of Ireland and his youth. His
memories, once they were aglow,
disclosed those bright colors of
romance which seem to linger forever in Irish breasts like the many
hues in an opal, though it is dull
enough until touched by light.

As he told of Christmas in his
childhood's land, he drew up his

hoe until the handle raised his arm
above his head, "restin' his rheu-
matiz," and so talked on of how
once he saw Gipsies — the queen
of Gipsies, in fact, if his cred-
ulous boyhood was not deceived
by great earrings, and a profusion
of black hair, and a crimson head-
cloth, and a broad bracelet. It
was a green Christmas that year,
and he met a man in a lane who
said, "Come with me and the Gipsy
queen will give you a Christmas gift
for your mother, my lad."

He was just beginning to tell me
what happened before he saw his
mother again — before she threw
her arms around her lost boy
"weepin' fur jaiy" — when he
stopped to gaze at a passing street
car.

"There it is, sir — the sign that
set me thinkin' of it all!" He
squinted hard, pointing with the
hand whereon was the brass ring. I
saw the word *Gipsy* in big letters

ONCE HE SAW THE QUEEN OF THE
GYPSIES

on a placard attached to the car's end, and understood its meaning at once. Denis McShane's old eyes had been unable to make out the smaller lettering, and I explained that a Gipsy missioner was addressing crowds every night down in the city.

"A sure 'nough Gipsy?"

"So they say, Mr. McShane."

"Bedad, I'd like to set my eyes on wone o' thim fellers ag'in! 'Twould mind me o' me baiyhood, sure — an' maybe it *might* give me the feel o' me mother's arms once more."

The appeal of such words was irresistible. I forthwith proposed that we go together to hear the Gipsy missioner. I trust Father O'Leary not to blame me, if this confession should ever reach his experienced ears. For nothing was further from my mind just then than desire to turn Denis from the faith of his fathers.

So eager was he that we went that very night. The meeting was

in a vast hall. Denis had no spe-
cial cause for misgivings on the
score of entering a church, for the
masses of people filling floor and
galleries were scurrying for seats
or chatting with vivacious expect-
ancy; and besides that, at sight of
those circling balconies Denis re-
called the pleasure of more than
one Democratic rally or convention
in that dazzling auditorium. He felt
quite at home and bore himself
accordingly — having found seats
by the front railing in a top gallery,
my old Irishman promptly fixed his
hat in the holder under his seat and
leaned forward to enjoy looking
down on the crowd.

A chorus massed high back of
the rostrum was rolling out song
after song with dramatic rendition.
Presently the precentor turned to
the throng of listeners and called,
"All sing that chorus!" Led by
his waving arm the multitude broke
into a surge of song like the voice of

many waters. Denis straightened
up and crossed himself brow and
breast.

"Now you sing it alone up there,
friends!" The leader swept with
his gesture a long side gallery as if
he were summoning inhabitants of
Mars. "That gallery is usually
almost as good as the choir" — he
paused to look round on his chorus
playfully — "come on, the rest of us
will listen, then we'll all sing it after
you. Come on — now — *sing!*"

From the high slope thus utilized
a brave but somewhat imponderous
attempt was made to meet the chal-
lenge, every ear and eye attentive.
Denis joined good-naturedly in the
general ripple of laughter. And
when, like a commander proudly
ordering up his whole army to over-
whelm some slight repulse, the leader
cried, "Ev–rybody, sing it!" in
the joyous roar of song I heard
beside me the responsive voice of
Denis catching at the words,

At the Crossing

"At the cross, at the cross, where I first
    saw the light,
    And the burden of my heart rolled
    away."

But it must be admitted that there was "niver a bit of a tyune," indeed, even as he had said.

These things were only preparatory, however. All were aware of this, including my companion.

"Where's the Gipsy?" he asked at length in a tone heard by others besides myself. A multitude of singing angels with harps would hardly have turned his mind from that question much longer.

"There he comes — see?"

Denis peered under his hand.

A man was making his way among the occupants of the platform — quiet, alert, greeting one and another fraternally.

He emerged at the front, stood serene, swept the throng with brooding eyes, lifted his hand — and in

the stillness that came we heard,
"Let us pray."

As I bowed my head I saw Denis
crossing himself again.

The prayer was brief, tender, ap-
pealing. When it ended we saw the
same figure standing as before. He
was rather short but of strong build;
his sturdy head was mantled with
long black hair; a Roman nose and
an ample black mustache gave dis-
tinct outlines to his face even at our
distance. But more than all else
his voice was masterful. For res-
onant sweetness and the tone of
authority, it was wonderful.

"Where's the Gipsy?" Denis
whispered it this time.

"That man — the one in front."
Remembering his poor eyes, I added,
"The man whose voice we just
heard."

Denis smiled his incredulity as
one does who has private knowledge
of a matter.

The missioner was speaking aside

to those about him. Soon he turned
and announced that he would sing
himself now — he had been listening to our songs, he said.

A piano was softly touched, a
hush fell on the assembly, and the
Gipsy's voice rose like a bird taking
wing in still air—gliding—circling
— poising — heaven-going —

"I—will sing—the won–drous sto–o–ry
   Of—the Christ—who di–ied—for me,
  How—he left—his home—in glo–o–ry
   For—the cross—on Cal–va–ry."

The multitude was listening like
a little child as he went on telling
"the wondrous story" —

"I—was lost—but Jesus—found me,
   Found—the sheep—that went astray,
  Threw—his loving—ar–rms—around me,
   Drew—me back—into–o—his way."

On reaching the refrain a second
time the singer lifted his hand, saying softly, "Sing with me!" And
like a sea-chant indeed rose the voice
of the people in swelling cadence,

With Denis McShane

"Yes, I'll sing—the won–drous sto–o–ry
  Of—the Christ—who di–ied—for me,
Sing it—with—the sa–aints—in glo-
      o–o–ry,
    Gath–ered by—the crys–tal sea."

Such unison of many voices in a
quavering Welsh tune, so great a
host borne upward by the simplest
words as it were by wings — all
under the spell of a single gentle
voice and lifted hand — it was mar-
velous to watch. But it well nigh
failed to interest Denis. Not until
the gliding mass of voices rose to
that line at the refrain's end,

"Sing it—with—the sa–aints—in glo-
      o–o–ry,"

did his face show any sign.of appre-
ciation. I think it was disbelief
or at least doubt as to the missioner's
genuine gipsyhood that threw him
into irresponsiveness.

Presently some one read the narrative of the boy Jesus being missed

by his mother as she was returning home from the temple. Another song was sung — it was "I need Thee every hour" — then the missioner began to talk.

I have never been good at remembering sermons, but the Gipsy's seems fairly clear even now as I try to recall it. His theme was *The Lost Christ*. As he pictured the mother's anxiety about her lost boy, he caught the ear of Denis at once. The old man leaned forward, squinting hard and gazing. Before long he turned to say, "I bet he *is* wone o' thim fellers! That's like 'em — lost childer' an' mothers huntin' 'em, an' all that." Then I heard him talking to himself as he again leaned over the railing to listen.

"She lost Christ, friends, as she was going away from the church," sounded the missioner's voice.

"Sure — the darlin'!" lisped Denis. "But the Holy Mother couldn't help that, now — 'twas some o' thim

Jew fellers kep' 'im, talkin' to 'im an' sich — jus' like Gipsies does."

"She sought him," the preacher next declared, "among her friends and kinsfolk, but she did not find him there."

"Sure — sure! He's Gipsy —he knows 'bout that all right — how mothers hunts an' can't find 'em!" So I heard Denis muse.

While the missioner pressed his point home to the social foibles and Christless relations of us all, the old man at the high gallery rail kept repeating, "Sure!—Sure!" But I could not make out clearly whether it was the absence of Christ in our lives or the presence of a Gipsy, a real Gipsy, then and there, that he was so certain about.

Finally, speaking with winning skill, the preacher reached the climax. "She found him, friends, where she had lost him — found him when she went back to the temple, seeking *Him*."

I felt the force of this expository artistry, this mesmeric humanness — felt it gripping my own possibly too careless spirit. Yet I was even more concerned just then to learn what Denis would make of that point.

His face, bent low over the railing, was all abeam. I saw glistening at the eyes — with the back of his ring hand he stayed a trickle or two. Then he turned his shaggy countenance to mine.

"Bedad, he *is* Gipsy! He knows their ways all right. Thim Jew fellers would niver 'av' done it, though — niver 'av' give 'er a sight o' him — but fur hearin' that a lot o' folks wuz out huntin' the dear lad. That's the Gipsy way, you see — he knows."

"She found him," sounded the preacher's voice pleadingly, "when she came back where she had lost him."

"Sure! Sure!" murmured the

voice at the gallery rail. "I knows how it wuz."

Presently, drawn by persuasive tenderness, men and women and youth who "wanted to come back where they lost Him" were moving all over the hall, going forward to stand before the missioner. Denis looked on with silent gaze.

Soon I observed that he was working off the brass ring. Then, furtively, under the cover of his hand, he peered at the Gipsy *through the ring.*

On our way home my companion recognized an acquaintance of his in the car, one Devlin — Pat Devlin — a boxer of repute whom I had not the pleasure of knowing before. Him I ventured to ask for his impression as to the Gipsy.

" 'Taint fair!" was his ungloved return. When I inquired why he took that view, he replied, "He sung me guards down, an' then he punched me."

At the Crossing

But my only regret when our "good night" words were said was that I had not heard to the end the story of Denis and the Gipsies long ago.

IV

WHEN CHRISTMAS CAME

THE next day was wet and dismal. I did not go far from our blazing˜fireplace. But through the windows I saw Denis pass the house at his work sometime late in the afternoon.

On the following morning I strolled out in the winter sunshine hoping to meet my friend. I wanted to hear the rest of that story. Instead, I heard shocking news.

The evening before Denis McShane had been run over. In the dark day's early nightfall, it appeared, while the old man was plodding at his task, amid vehicles hurrying home, he had failed to see or hear an automobile in time. He was bruised — would be confined

to his bed for some time — it was
hoped that there were no fatal
injuries — that was all anybody
could tell me.

I saw Denis before the turn of
the day set in; and no weather kept
me from his door as the shortening
days sped us toward Christmastide.
He was always cheerful in spite of
pain and distressing weakness.

But do what we might, there was
no rallying of his vital powers. The
shock had been too much for his
age-worn frame. The silver cord
was loosed, the golden bowl broken,
the pitcher broken at the fountain,
the wheel broken at the cistern
—the mechanism that drew life's
waters for him would work no more.

When the bells of Christmas Eve
began to sound, we saw that the end
was near. His ear caught their
music still; and he smiled, welcom-
ing the merry clangor — he whose
heart had been set on not "feeling
too old for Christmas."

[48]

With Denis McShane

"Thim minds me o' the way I used to shpring out o' me bed — when the wone bell we had would r-i-ng, r-i-ng, startin' Christmas — in County Galway — in me baiyhood." Pain caught his voice at times, pain in his left side; but his countenance quickly shone again afterward.

"I feels the touch o' the floor on wone foot now — jus' wone, though — 'twas a earth floor — an' I sees the path o' moonlight I stepped in — to git sight — o' the first peep o' day."

Then he lay for a while with eyes closed; and his face was as when mortals smile in a happy dream.

As the night deepened Father O'Leary came. And by his kindness the Domine, when he called at the door, entered and remained in the house.

Father O'Leary was with the sufferer alone for a time. I suppose that the soul of Denis eased itself
[49]

of all cumber then — man's ear and voice making God's real for such a one as he. And somehow, I doubt not, the Sin-bearer was known of him, giving much the same solace that I hope for when my time comes.

At length Father O'Leary beckoned the Domine and me into the little bedroom. Denis had something he wished to have us hear. The door being shut, Father O'Leary held in his hand the brass ring that Denis wore. And thus he spoke

"Mr. McShane is grateful to you for the long friendship you have shown him. Therefore he wishes you to hear the story of this ring — and what follows it."

The priest spoke like one fulfilling a trust with simple fidelity.

"When he was a lad in Ireland he was led away to a Gipsy camp. There a woman who made him believe she was the queen of Gipsies talked with him. She took up a ring and, fixing her eyes upon him,

[50]

looked at him through the ring.
While she did this she said, as he
remembers her words,

> 'Through something round
> His fate is found.'

She added some saying about
'bound,' but he can not recall that."

Denis turned his head on the
pillow, opened his eyes wide, then
squinted them to scan our faces.

"A hue and cry was raised for
the lost boy, and neighbors joined
in hunting for him. Because of
this the boy was returned to a place
near his mother's cottage whence
he had been led away. But, being
made to believe that the woman's
ring held the secret of his destiny,
he had contrived to steal it and
bear it away. This is that Gipsy
ring.

"He kept it, a secret treasure. At
first he imagined that the 'something
round' which the Gipsy woman saw
through this ring might be the coin

of the realm — that he was to prosper by making money. In this hope he came to America. When the Civil War broke out, and he enlisted as a soldier, in battle or on picket duty he feared that a bullet might be the 'something round' that would determine his fate. After the war was over, when he married Mrs. McShane he hoped and believed that the marriage ring was what the Gipsy woman claimed to see through this ring; and he wishes to bear testimony to the blessings she brought into his life."

Denis made a sound, and we saw that he wished to speak. We bent over him. A light as of rapture flooded the old countenance. We all heard him say, "The darlin'! — I'm goin' to her, Father."

So simple, so genuine was it all that it was hard for us, men though we were, to master our emotions before such a tribute to love's memory and longing. Father O'Leary's eyes were wet behind his glasses — wet with tears as human as ours. But not a quiver touched the stanch little priest's voice.

"When he got the job of — of caretaker in the street" — that euphemism's quick tenderness somehow well nigh unmanned me — "he had a fear that the wheels of some vehicle might bring to pass what the Gipsy woman had said. He was always on guard against them — more than ever apprehensive when automobiles began to appear in the street having wheels that seemed to steal upon him in swift silence."

Not once, such was the kindness of Father O'Leary, did any sign escape him betraying recognition of humor in such fancies. After all, it must have been very much like our heavenly Father's way with us in taking our work-a-day fears with serious sympathy — most of them, at any rate.

"An' wone o' thim," Denis mur-

mured, "wone o' thim shtill quick
wheels — wuz it, sure 'nough — at
last."

We heard the Christmas bells
ring out once more. It was mid-
night. The little house-clock, whir-
ring and noisily thrumming twelve
strokes, left no doubt of that.

"Merry Christmas — to yese —
an' to everybody!" softly sounded
from the bed.

"The Lord be with thee," said
the pastor.

"An' wid thy spirit, Father."

Then Father O'Leary turned to
the Domine. "You have been a
good friend to him, and he wishes
that you should join me in executing
a Christmas trust for him — his
farewell to the world." Gently
reaching under the pillow Father
O'Leary drew forth a knotted small
bag.

"You wish that we should use
these savings of yours for the hap-
piness of little children who are

WE TOOK OUR WAY HOME

not likely to have Christmas gifts tomorrow — dividing the money equally between us?"

"Would that be all right wid you, Father?"

"Certainly. It would give me a very happy Christmas."

"Then I do — as you jus' said it."

"I will gladly accept such a trust," said the Domine. And he clasped Father O'Leary's hand. The two men stood thus, looking down on Denis.

An ashen whiteness had overcast his face. The gleam of peace was shining there still; but how pallid was its light!

Father O'Leary turned and began the last rites.

When the soul of Denis had departed, others having come into the room the Domine and I joined with all our hearts in the final Responsitory, nothing being therein to give us pause.

Sweet to us was the opening

call, "Come to his assistance, ye saints of God, come forth to meet him, ye angels of the Lord: Receiving his soul: Offering it in the sight of the Most High." Sweeter still was the petition, "May Christ receive thee, who hath called thee." Beautiful in our ears were the words, "Eternal rest grant unto him, O Lord, and let perpetual light shine upon him."

So we went on together, until Father O'Leary's voice sounded at last alone, "Tibi, Domine, commendamus" — "To Thee, O Lord, do we commend the soul of Thy servant Denis McShane, that being dead to the world he may live unto Thee; and whatsoever sins he has committed through the frailty of his mortal nature, do Thou, by the pardon of Thy merciful love, wash away."

The Domine and I said *Amen* with the others.

And the "Passing Bell" that rang

LITTLE ONES OF THE POOR BUBBLING
OVER WITH GLADNESS

for Denis in the tower of St. Anne's
no doubt seemed to the townsfolk
in their dreams the bells of Christmas
ringing still!

As we took our way home, Father
O'Leary said, "We can not always
see eye to eye in matters of faith,
but we can in the things of love."

"And of hope," answered the Domine; "we are together in two of
the great three, anyway."

When Christmas Day came, there
were little ones of the poor, both
Catholic and Protestant, who were
bubbling over with gladness at pretty
gifts that came from the First Church
parsonage and from the rectory of
St. Anne's. Sometimes the dividing lines got crossed. The Dave
Shaw children could hardly believe
that their presents came from Father
O'Leary; and Bridget Walsh said,
"Well now, that's handsome!" when
she found that the things for her
little ones had come from the Domine.

But by and by they all got it straightened out and understood that Denis McShane was the source of their Christmas joy.

"After all," said I to the Domine as we sat together that night, speaking of the small coins which made up the bag of savings, "after all, the Gipsy queen's words came true in a better sense than that of the wheels —

> ' Through something round
> His fate is found.' "

"I was thinking," the dear man answered, gazing into the bright fireplace, "I was thinking — how the last crossing Denis swept clean is on the highway that leads us all to our Father's House."

CPSIA information can be obtained at www.ICGtesting.com
Printed in the USA
BVOW11s1024120814

362576BV00035B/1044/P